Fire Truck

nuts and bolts

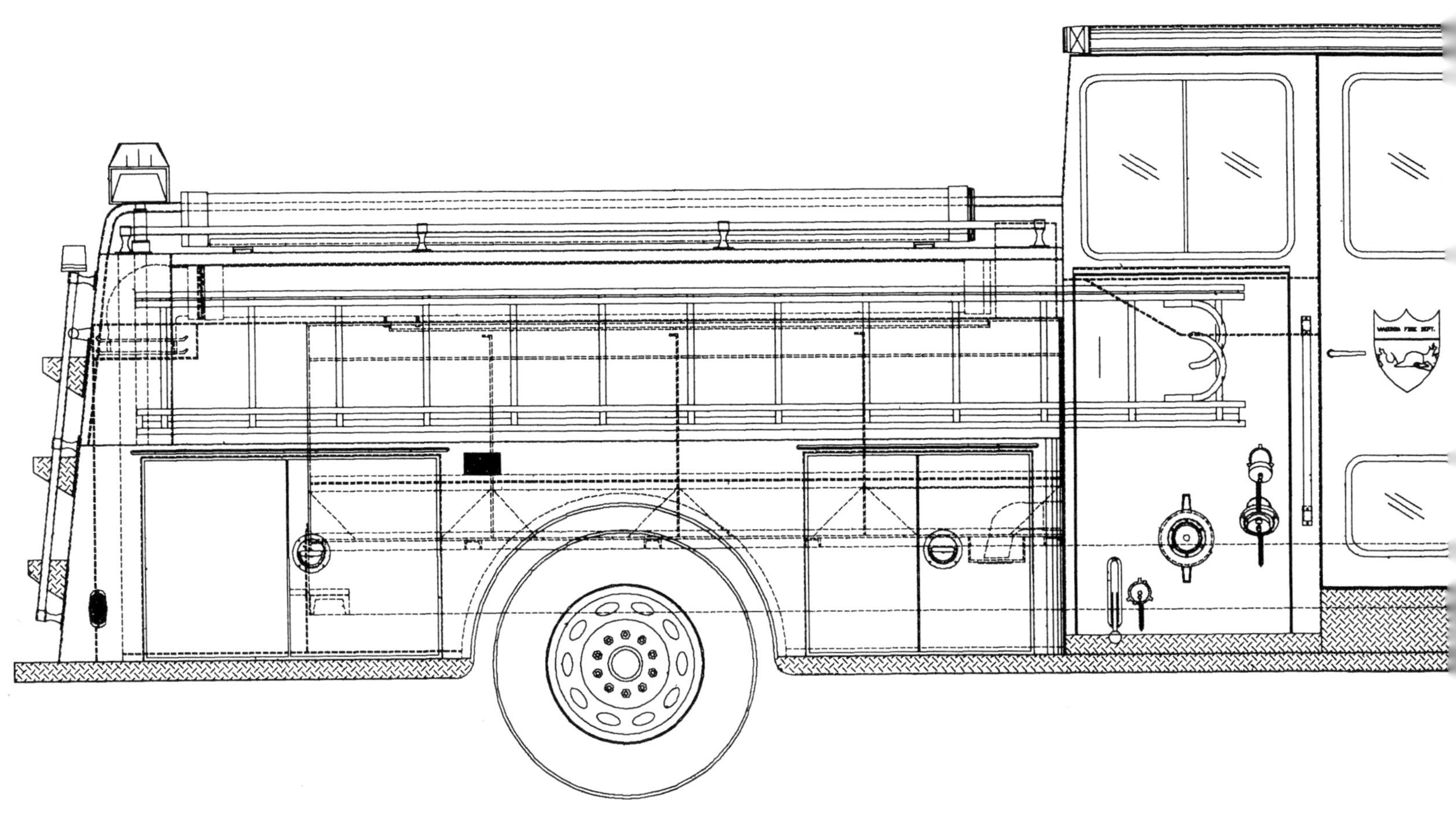

Fire Truck

nuts and bolts

by Jerry Boucher

with a foreword by Jim Kirvida
of Custom Fire Apparatus, Inc.

Carolrhoda Books, Inc./Minneapolis

To Mitch Kirvida

All photographs are by the author, except for the following, which are reproduced courtesy of: pp. 6-7, Timothy P. Snopek; pp. 21 (both), 23 (bottom left), 24 (both), Joe Heitzinger.

This book is available in two editions:
Library binding by Carolrhoda Books, Inc.
Soft cover by First Avenue Editions
c/o The Lerner Group
241 First Avenue North
Minneapolis, MN 55401

LIBRARY OF CONGRESS CATALOGING-IN-PUBLICATION DATA

Boucher, Jerry, 1941-
Fire truck nuts and bolts / Jerry Boucher.
p. cm.
Summary: Follows the steps involved in building a pumper fire engine, from choosing the cab and chassis through adding special features and painting to testing and delivery.
ISBN 0-87614-783-X (lib. bdg.)
ISBN 0-87614-619-1 (pbk.)
1. Fire engines—Design and construction—Juvenile literature. [1. Fire engines—Design and construction.] I. Title.
TH9372.B68 1993
629.255—dc20 92-37476
CIP
AC

Manufactured in the United States of America
3 4 5 6 7 – P/MP – 01 00 99 98 97 96

For Metric Conversion

When you know:	multiply by:	to find:
length		
inches	2.54	centimeters
feet	30.48	centimeters
weight		
pounds	.45	kilograms
tons	.91	metric tons
capacity		
gallons	3.79	liters

FOREWORD

by Jim Kirvida, President
Custom Fire Apparatus

Building fire trucks isn't something you can learn in school—not in formal schools at least. The art of fire truck building is handed down from generation to generation. Today's fire truck builders use modern tools but never forget the craft skills that have been passed down to them.

Fire trucks are the result of many hours of detailed planning, design, and hand-building. Designs are constantly being upgraded as new fire fighting technologies, new highway standards, and new construction materials, such as stainless steel, are introduced. Modern fire trucks are built so that they can be easily taken apart and modified to meet changing needs.

In the following pages, you will see how our small midwestern company, Custom Fire Apparatus, meets the demands of modern fire safety. Being a small, hands-on builder means being able to work closely with every customer. We listen to fire fighters and design to meet their special needs.

The pumper truck shown in this book required 1,670 hours of labor to construct. Because our company builds only an average of 36 trucks and other vehicles each year, we consider each truck to be not only a unique construction project but also a work of art.

WAUKESHA
ENGINE
1
LIFE
PROPERTY

Fire trucks are all different from each other, but they all have one thing in common. They help put out fires and save lives. In this book, we're going to watch a fire truck being built. We will follow our truck through all the steps from planning to delivery.

On a bright fall morning, members of a small town fire department are meeting with the owner of a fire truck company. They are talking over the kind of truck they want to have built. Each fire truck is built to meet the special needs of the fire department buying the truck.

How many fire fighters will the truck carry? How many feet of hose will it hold? Will there be ladders on both sides of the truck? All of these questions must be answered before a truck can be built.

The company makes many kinds of fire apparatus, as fire trucks are called. Our truck is a pumper truck. It won't bend in the middle or have tall platforms with high, extending ladders. Pumper trucks are built to pump water onto fires.

The fire department chooses a cab and frame, also called the chassis. The chassis arrives at the fire truck company with nothing on it. The company's skilled workers will build our truck right onto the chassis out of parts they make themselves and parts they buy from other companies.

Workers will take this ▼

and turn it into this. ▲

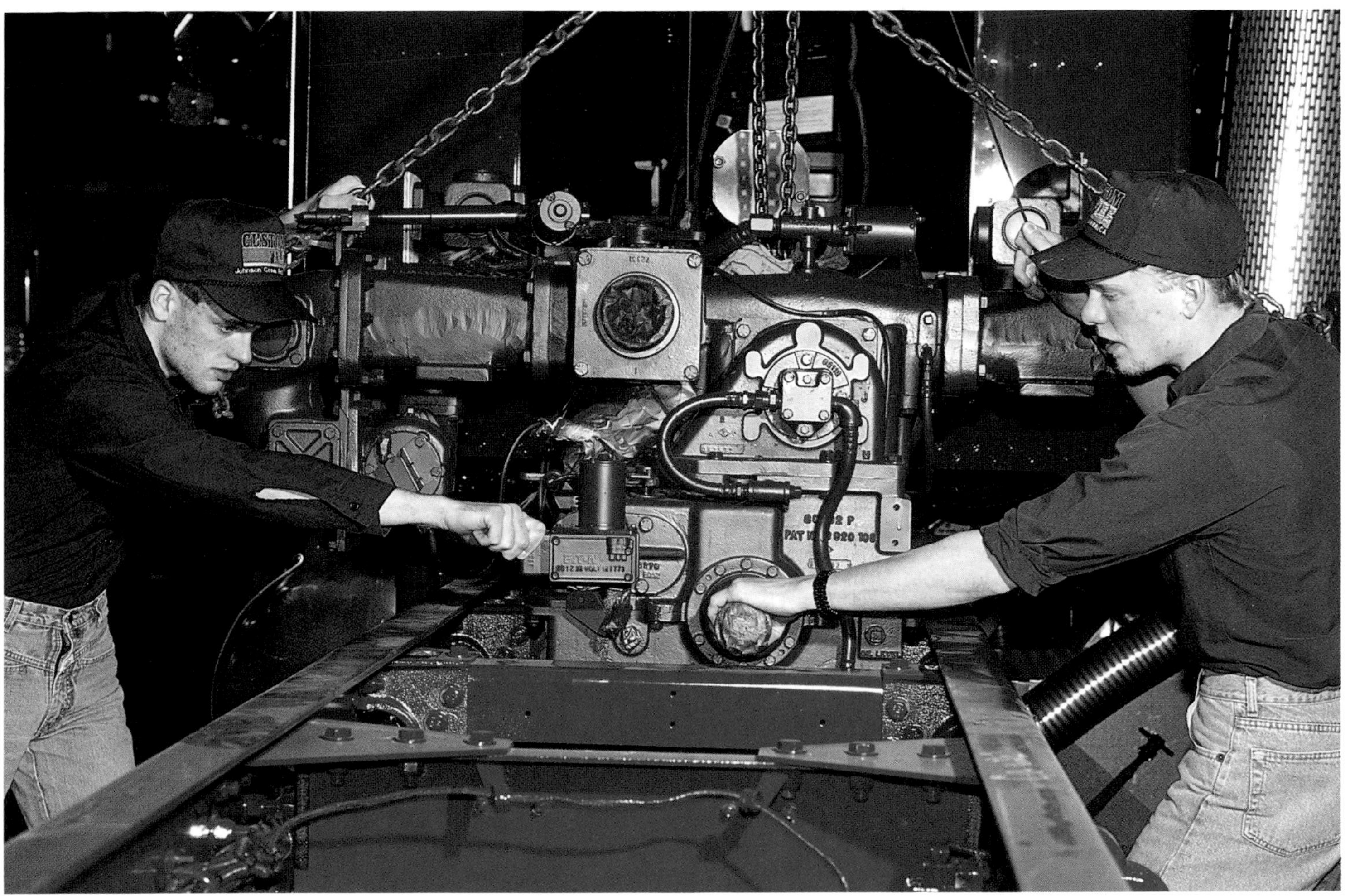

The first thing put on the chassis is a water pump. The water pump, also called a fire pump, is the heart of the truck. It's what makes this truck a fire truck.

Before the water pump was added, our truck's drive shaft had to be changed. The drive shaft usually takes power from the engine to the back wheels. In our truck, the drive shaft will be able to send power either to the water pump or to the back wheels, but not to both. This fire truck can't be moving and pumping water at the same time.

With the pump in place, a worker adds valves, controls, outlets, and connections. These add-ons differ from truck to truck.

Our truck already has a frame behind the cab. But workers also build and add a subframe. The subframe will support the body and water tank that are going to be built. A fire truck's subframe holds up a fire truck the way a bed frame supports a mattress.

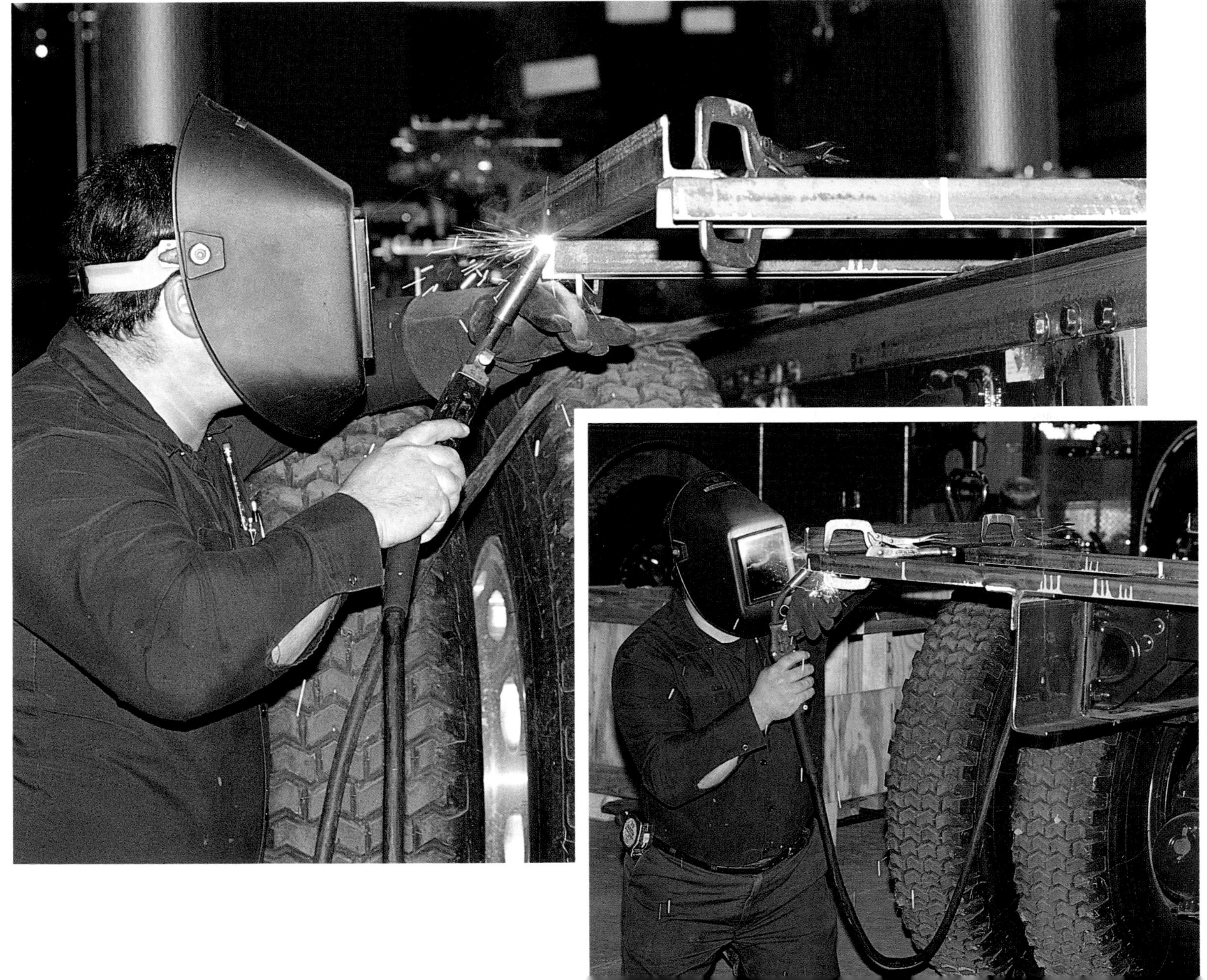

The manager looks over the plans many times during the building of the truck. Each step has to be done exactly as the plans show. Many different people work on the truck and all of them must do their part right for the finished truck to turn out as it was designed.

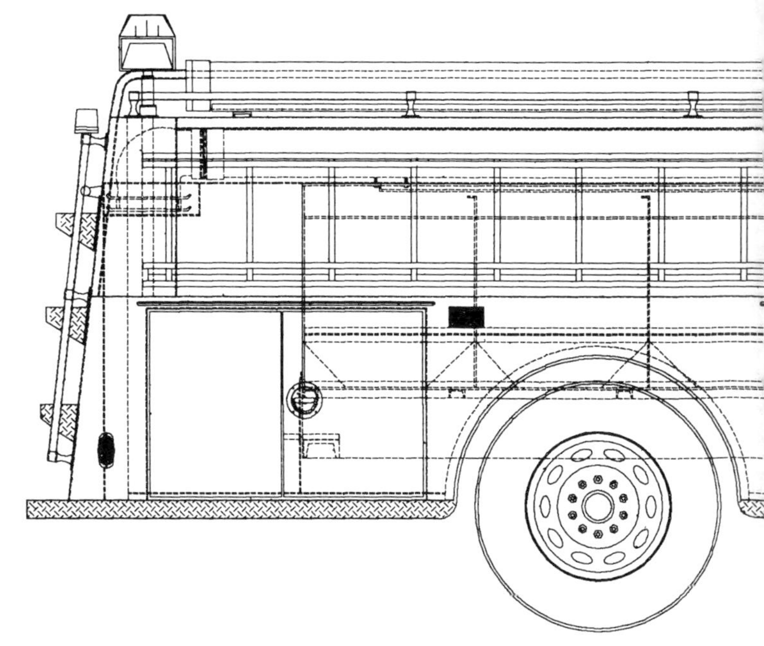

CUSTOM FIRE	WEIGHTS: LOADED	DIMENSIONS: OVERALL
	FRONT: 12,500 lbs.	LENGTH: 32' 9"
	REAR: 23,500 lbs.	WIDTH: 101"
	TOTAL: 36,000 lbs.	HEIGHT: Cab 122" (129)
	DATE: 9/25/90	FOR: WACONIA

CHASSIS: Peterbilt 375	BODY STYLE: Full Resp.	FIRE PUMP: Wat. CS-1500
ENGINE: 3306-300 hp	WATER TANK: 1,000 GALS.	CAPACITY: 1,500 GPM
WHEELBASE: 245"	HOSEBED CAP: 900', 5"	SUCTIONS: 3-6", 2-2.5"
CAB-TO-AXLE: 162"	800', 3" 500' 1.75"	DISCHARGES: 6-2.5", 3-3.5"
DRAWN BY: Len Kirvida	DRAWING NO.: 1WM90	SCALE: 1"=10'

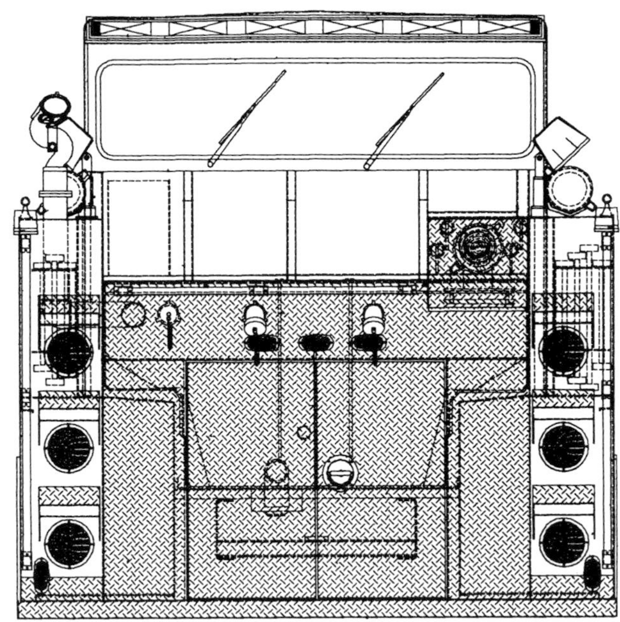

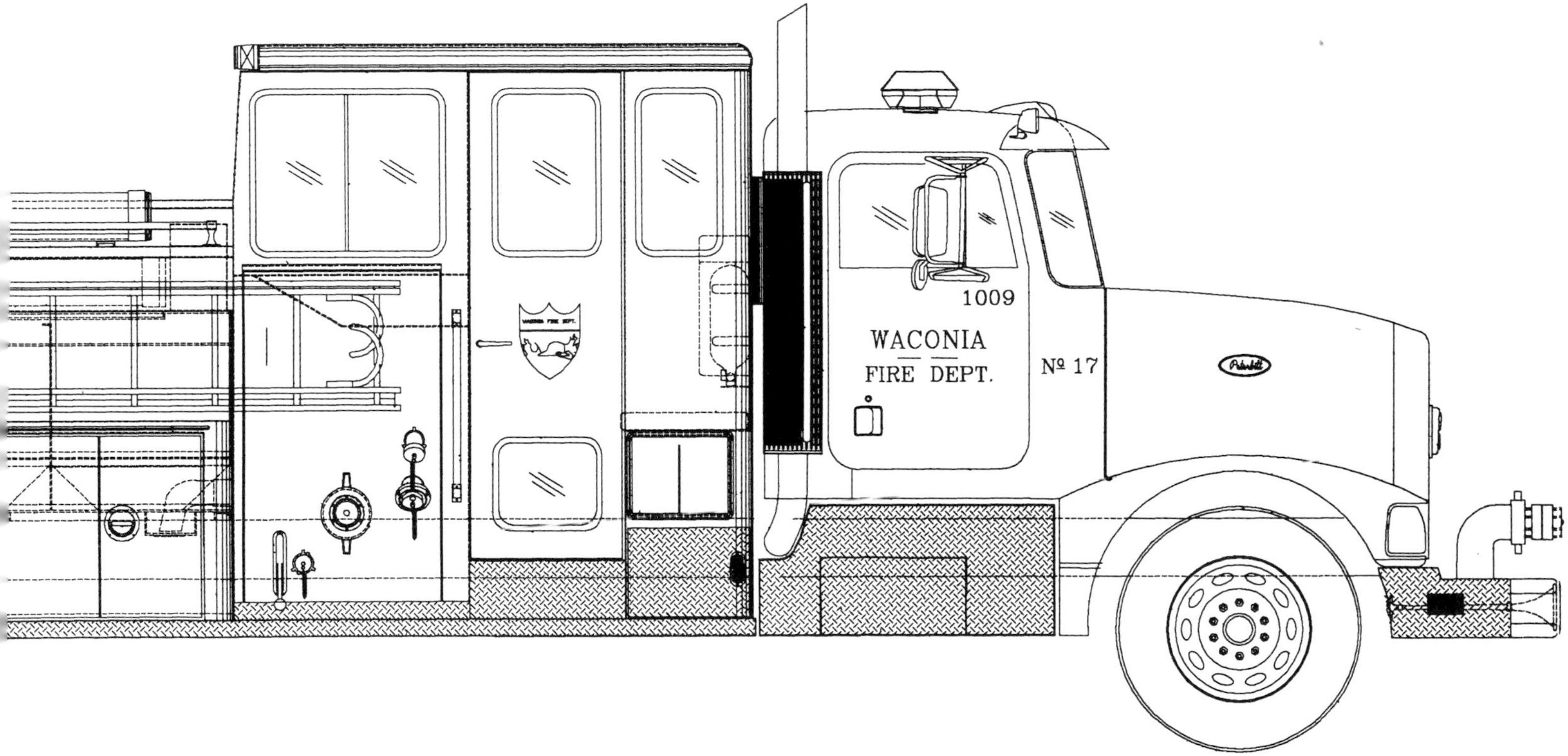

1009

WACONIA
FIRE DEPT.

№ 17

Before the body can be built, the frame and subframe are painted. This will protect the metal from being eaten away by water and road salts.

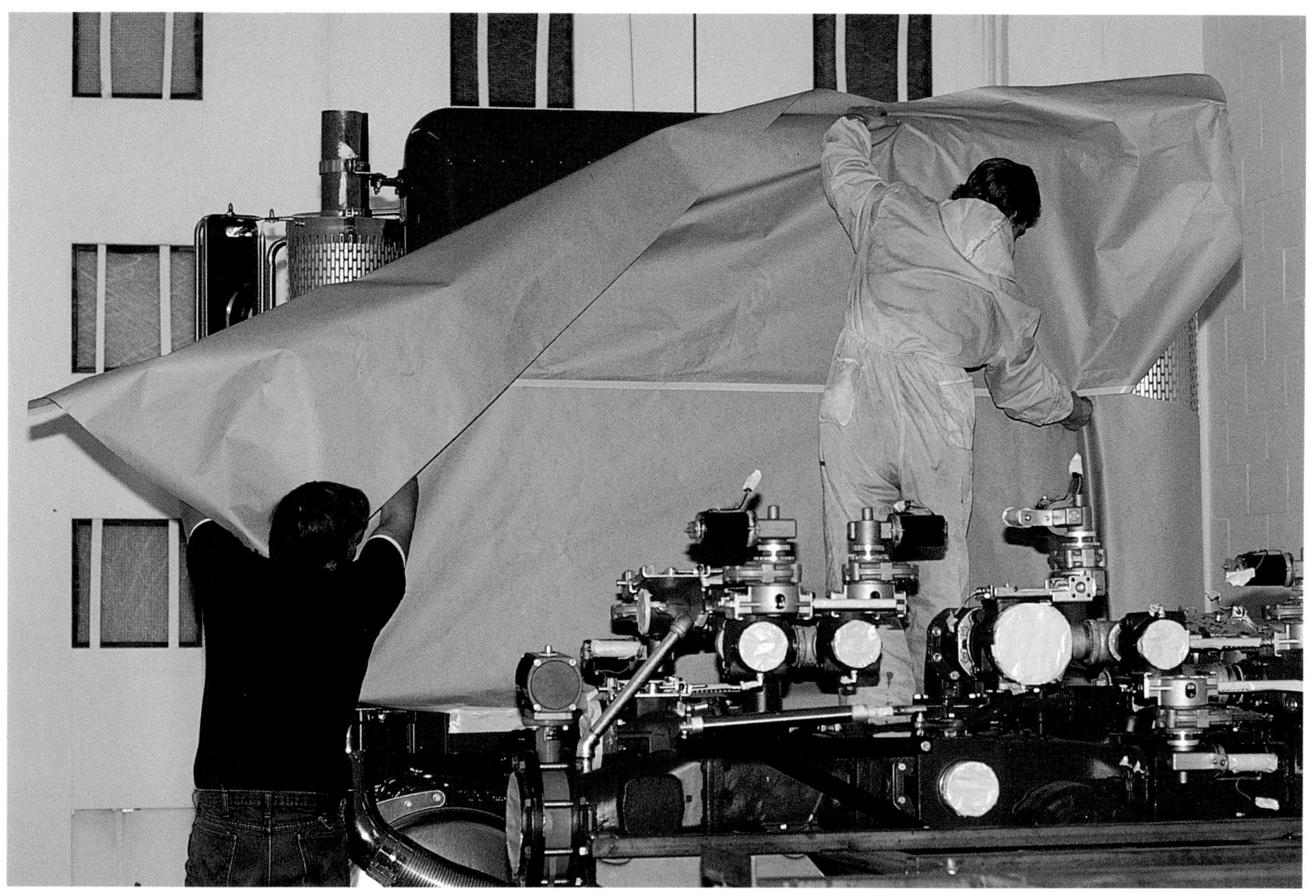

First the cab is wrapped in paper and plastic.

Then the paint guns spray paint . . .

. . . until every inch is covered.

Now workers can begin to build the body. The body is like the shell of the truck. It is made from sheets of metal, each 1/8 inch thick. That's twice as thick as the metal used for cars.

About 16 sheets of metal will make a finished fire truck. Each sheet is 6 feet by 12 feet, about as long and wide as a small station wagon.

A great deal of craftsmanship goes into making the truck body. Workers use very few machines and tools to turn the flat metal sheets into a beautifully crafted fire truck.

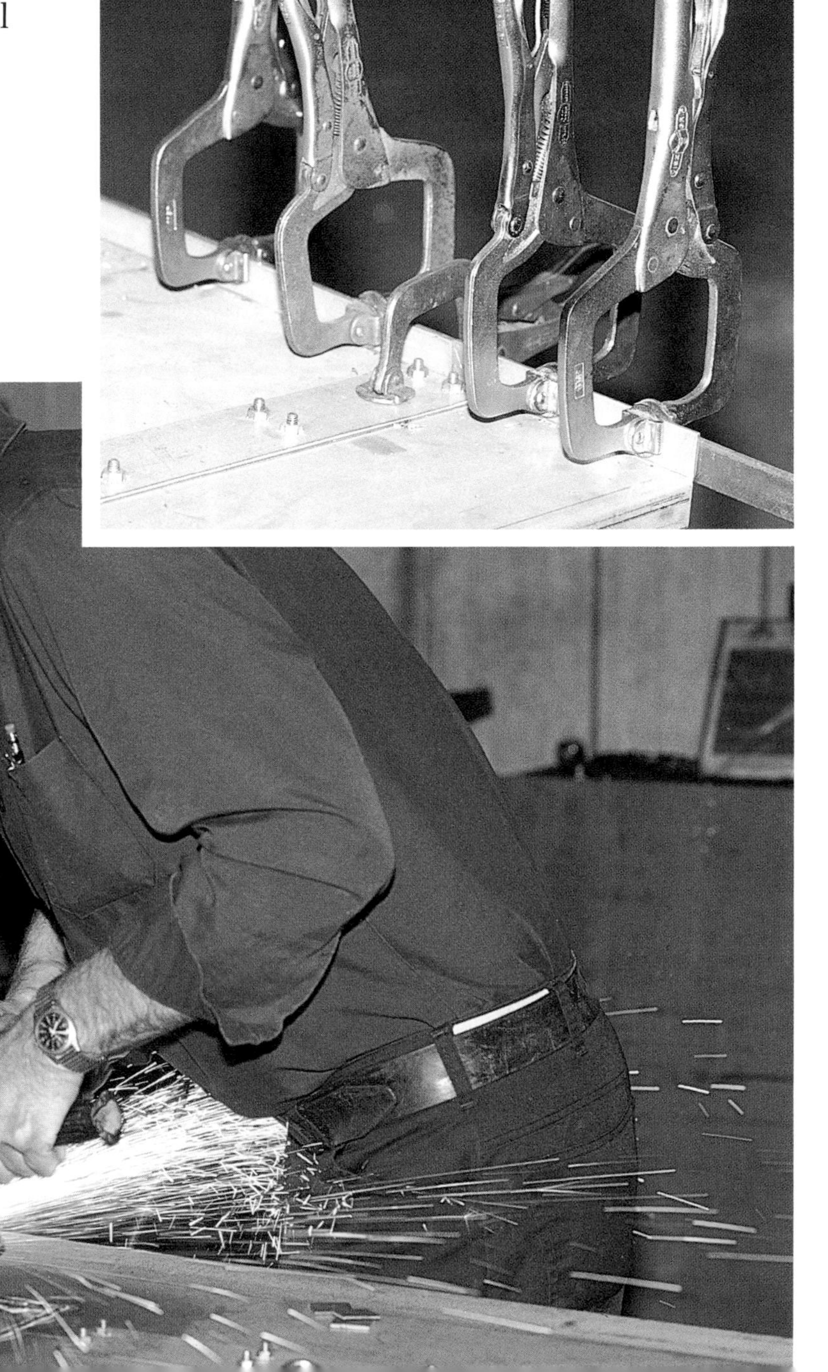

The two largest machines used are the shearer, which cuts metal sheets down to size, and the press brake. The press brake uses about 225 tons of pressure to bend and shape the metal.

First one, and then another, panel is being set in place on either side of the truck.

Each side panel will have compartments of different sizes and shapes to hold the fire department's tools and supplies.

Ladder racks are built onto the side panels. These ladders come right off the truck. When extended, they will reach three stories.

Behind the truck cab, the Full Response cab is taking shape. This cab will have room for four fire fighters. It will also contain the truck's controls and gauges.

Fire trucks must carry some water with them. This allows some of the truck's crew members to start fighting a fire as soon as they arrive on the scene. Other fire fighters get the truck's hoses connected to a water source, such as a hydrant or a lake.

A 1,000-gallon water tank, called a booster tank, is being set in place in our truck. Once the tank is in place, it will be covered by the rest of the truck's body. The fire hoses are usually stored above the water tank when they aren't being used.

Work goes on until the body is completed.

Now our truck is ready to be painted. But before the truck gets a full paint job, all the doors and other parts that can be taken off are removed. They will be painted separately.

The cab and chrome parts that can't be removed are carefully covered. Then the rest of the truck gets its first coat.

This first coat is called primer. The white primer coat helps later coats of paint stay on the metal body. If the truck didn't get a coat or two of primer, the paint would chip and flake off later.

Preparing and painting one of these trucks are big tasks. A painter and an assistant work hard to get the job done. Cleaning, sanding, buffing, and painting the truck body and parts take almost 150 hours. It takes about an hour to put on each coat of paint. Our truck will get two coats of primer and three coats of color.

Most fire trucks are red. They may look as if they are all the same color, but they are really painted in many different shades of red.

After being painted, our truck is put back together. Now it's ready to be finished.

Lights,

trim,

wires, ladders, gauges, panels, and many, many other parts are added at this time.

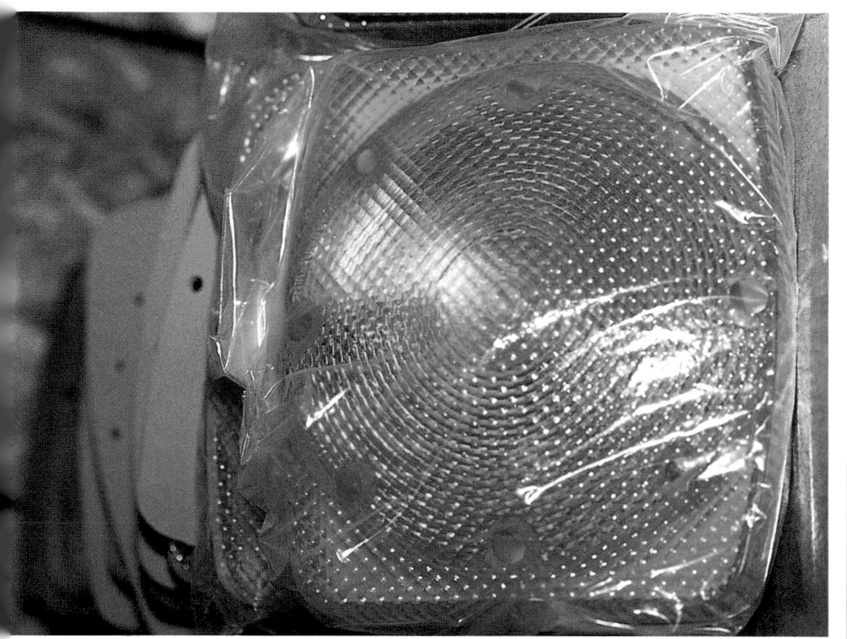

Some of these parts were made by companies that specialize in making hoses, valves, and other parts. The fire truck company often orders parts in large numbers and in many different sizes.

Gauges and switches in the Full Response cab will tell the fire fighters how fast the engine is running, how hot it is, how much water the pump is pumping, and how much pressure is going through each hose. By looking at these gauges, the fire fighters will know exactly how the truck is performing during a fire.

More parts are bolted in place.

More wires are connected.

Finally, only the light bar is left to be added. Workers set it in place on top of the truck cab, connect the wires, and tighten the last nuts and bolts. Once the light bar is in place, our fire truck is finished.

Members of the fire department have looked at the truck at different steps in its building. But this is their last time to inspect the truck. They look it over very carefully to be sure that they are pleased with every detail.

Once the fire fighters are completely happy with the truck, they are ready to call it their own. Their city's name is painted on the truck with real 24-karat gold leaf instead of gold paint. That extra detail says a lot about the quality built into fire trucks.

Fire trucks have to pass many tests before they can be delivered. Our truck is tested right at the fire truck company. Someone from Underwriters Laboratories, a testing group, watches as each test is done.

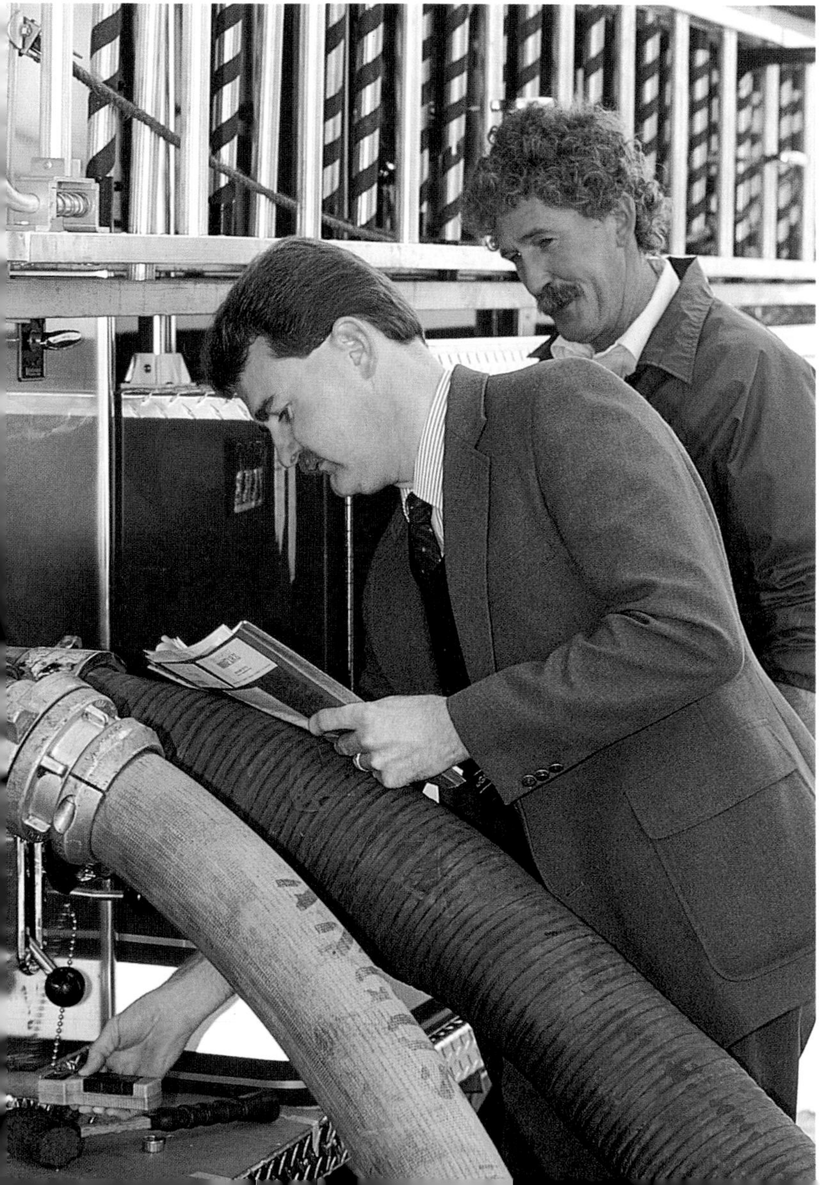

The tests last about three and one-half hours. At one point, our truck has to pump 1,500 gallons of water per minute for two full hours without stopping. The water comes out of the hoses at 150 pounds of pressure. It usually takes two or three strong fire fighters to hold onto a hose pumping at full force, but here the hoses are hooked up to the testing building. On the scene of a fire, the water can spray as far as 350 feet, more than the length of a football field.

The fire truck company has a large underground water tank just for the tests. Water is drawn out of the tank and then sprayed right back in so that it won't be wasted.

The fire fighters are back to pick up their truck. They load the fire hose onto the truck themselves.

It's time for the Waconia Fire Department to welcome its newest truck, Engine No. 17, to the station. The new pumper truck is joining the department's other fire trucks to protect the people and property of their town . . .

. . . while back at the fire truck company, the workers have already sorted out the nuts and bolts and other parts for the next fire truck.